ALL THAT MATTERS

TESSA RICE

COPYRIGHT INFORMATION

All That Matters

STONE COMPASS PRESS

www.StoneCompassPress.com

10 9 8 7 6 5 4 3 2 1

DEDICATION

This book is dedicated to my family, my friends, and the members of the

Hawaii Island Writers Association.

CHAPTER ONE

WESTERLY, RHODE ISLAND, 2030

I walked down the dark streets, a shopping bag clutched in one hand, huddling against the chill Rhode Island wind. The night was quiet, and I was anxious and more than a little afraid of the silence. Suddenly I heard soft footfalls behind me and was instantly on the alert. Not one, but three people, whom I would later discover were part of a mutant-hating group called the Exterminators. I stopped by a Honda Civic car, ready to throw it at my assailants if necessary. As a mutant, I had the strength, senses, exoskeleton, and mobility of an insect. I listened hard but heard nothing else. Snatching up my groceries, I practically ran the rest of the way home, all the while with the sense that I was not just being followed but watched. Dawn greeted me at the door, not noticing the way my hands were shaking. Julianne Worden, our foster mother, hailed me enthusiastically from the kitchen. Carter, her husband, was in his study, though he poked his head out to say hello. He was brown-haired and bespectacled, an interesting contrast to Julianne's sunny blonde looks. Dawn took the groceries and walked through the living room wall into the adjoining kitchen. Julianne, to her credit, didn't so much as blink at Dawn's ability to phase through solid objects. I didn't bother asking where Asher was; he was more than likely outside swimming in the pool. I managed a polite hello to the Lockwoods, Annette and Davis, and made dutiful small talk before heading outside. I sat in one of the lawn chairs, trying to arrange my long mahogany hair comfortably. Asher popped up and shot me a grin, his dark skin wet and scaly, drops of water clinging to his close-cropped black hair. I grinned back, choking on a laugh as he climbed out noisily; flashing me glimpses of his gills and webbed hands and feet. Asher heaved a satisfied sigh and flopped down next to me, purposely getting me wet. I gave him a swat that made him wince, but he smiled and hit me back.

"Hey, you two, dinner!" Dawn called out to us. Asher dried himself off, his skin slowly returning to normal, he and I slung an arm around each other's shoulders and walked inside. Dawn traded a look with Asher over the mashed potatoes, their identical liquid brown eyes glowing, and I saw him surreptitiously squeeze her hand.

And then I heard it again - the footfalls, and so I tensed, waiting to hear more.

"Tabby, what is it?" A frown creased Julianne's forehead.

"I thought I heard something. Sounded like feet."

"A cat, probably."

"No, it sounded like a person." I got up to go check.

Julianne took my wrist. "Tabby, hold on. Let's wait a few days, and if we hear it again, we'll report prowlers."

Carter set down his fork. "I don't think the police will be so keen to help us, honey."

Dawn stiffened; Asher looked down at his plate, but I saw the tightening of his jaw that indicated he was as frustrated as I felt. There was rarely a mention of the fact that my friends and I were mutants, but still, the snide voice in my head reminded me that the police were only human...unlike us. Annette tried to lighten the mood by asking about the new school being built. I seized on the subject gratefully, Dawn and Asher following suit. I relished the thought of the school like my mashed potatoes. As

Dawn and Asher cleared the table, I stood guard at the window, my ears straining to catch any hint of a trespasser.

"Hear anything?" Asher handed me a dish towel and stared outside, though he couldn't see a thing.

"No." I was disappointed and glad at the same time; of course I was happy that we were safe for the time being, but it would be nice to actually use my gift for something. I glanced out the window at our neighbors as they went back to their house across the street. Annette and Davis Lockwood were nice enough, but even they were nervous around us. I knew I shouldn't blame them, but then again, was it our fault my friends and I were so different? The kitchen was crowded with all of us doing the dishes, but we hardly noticed as we excitedly chattered about what the new school would be like. None of us knew that we would never get a chance to find out.

CHAPTER TWO

PROVIDENCE, THAT SAME NIGHT...

Darien raised the gun and shot the vampire squarely in the heart. Although still in his twenties, Darien was already an experienced hunter, his aim as accurate and deadly as his uncle's, who had been hunting since he was twenty-one.

Aldrich St. Albans, fifty-seven, mopped up another bloodsucker a few yards away. They had just trashed a nightclub housing vampires and were killing as many in sight as possible. Darien slashed and kicked and shot for all he was worth, thoughts of his half-vampire cousin making him even angrier. Aldrich let loose a hacking cough; Darien cut his way toward him and slung one of his uncle's arms around his neck.

"I'm gettin' too old for this." Aldrich rasped, clinging to his nephew's stocky, sinewy body. The thought of that made Darien cold inside and he pushed himself faster, dragging his uncle with him. They leaped into Darien's GTO and roared down the street, heading for their lair in Newport. Back at the dock house, Darien cleaned and sharpened his two short swords before reloading the guns. Aldrich had already gone to get some sleep, and it made Darien uneasy as he thought of his guardian no longer able to hunt down those who had destroyed his life. Unbidden an image came to him; a vision of his long-dead mother, her soft, dark brown eyes, eyes he saw every time he looked in the mirror. In his head he could hear her voice, always so calm. Darien shook his head fiercely; he wasn't Andre Stratton anymore. That name had died along with his parents. Darien, *Darien*, not Andre, went to his room and lay down, the last few harsh weeks catching up with him. In his room, Aldrich lay in bed. He was not asleep but looking at snapshots of his family; one in particular: a boy, no more than eleven, a huge smile on his face as he played soccer with Darien and an older boy, his half-brother Reece. Aldrich took another drag on his cigarette, blinking hard against the tears in his eyes. Above Aldrich, the same boy, Alain, now a human/vampire hybrid, sat on the roof watching his father. Alain pushed his flaxen hair out of his eyes, he knew he shouldn't be here, but he couldn't help himself. He had to see how Darien and especially Aldrich were doing. His eyes burned; he wanted to come home, but he couldn't. They wouldn't take him back, because of what he was now. Alain was so engrossed in watching his father he didn't even hear Darien come up behind him until he almost got a stake through the chest. Darien stared in total disbelief; the two young men faced one another for an instant, then Darien yanked out his gun and aimed straight at Alain's chest, where his heart was. Alain took a flying leap off the roof and hit the ground running. Shots rang out but Alain sprinted off into the night, unhurt and hoping that Aldrich wouldn't guess who had come and knowing that he probably would.

"Who was that?" Aldrich had heard the shots and came outside, although he had guessed who it was, and was angry with himself for being happy about it.

"Alain's back." Darien shoved his gun back in its holster, shaken by who he had seen...who he had almost shot to death. Darien grounded his teeth, pushing aside his misgivings; Alain was not his cousin, not anymore. Darien had told himself that a dozen times, and yet he felt sick inside at the shocked look on his uncle's face. Aldrich, for his part, knew the time would come when he would have to square off with Alain, for there was no cure for vampirism.

If it has to be done, Aldrich told himself, *then that's all there is to it.*

Darien watched his uncle closely, but Aldrich's inscrutable gaze made his feelings impossible to decipher. "Uncle Aldrich –"

"Darien, don't." Aldrich cut him off. Darien knew enough to shut up and let his uncle go back to bed. Aldrich shut the door, hard, and Darien went back to his own room, hoping that Alain would know enough not to come back here again.

SIX WEEKS LATER

AT THE PARK...

I shook my hair out of my face and pretended to chase Asher, who was grinning as he pelted me with another barrage of leaves. I laughed triumphantly as I tackled him and looped an arm around his neck. Asher yelped and squirmed, but he couldn't escape from my headlock.

"Give it up, pal. She's got you." An unfamiliar boy's voice cut into our wrestling match. I jumped to my feet as Dawn questioned the boy.

"Who are you?"

The boy, a tall Black teenager, made placating gesture with his hands. "Relax. We're not gonna hurt you guys."

"We?" I burst out. I turned slightly red as his eyes fixed on me for a second before gesturing behind him.

The boy smiled. "Yes, we. Us. My gang and me."

I watched in shock as several carbon copies of the boy came out from behind the trees and merged with the one standing in front of us.

"My name's Donaghan Case. You can call me Numberman. We're the Children of Eris. Also known as the Eris Gang." Donaghan gestured behind him, and more kids followed to cluster behind him, eyeing me and my friends with avid interest. Donaghan motioned to each of his friends in turn: Maiya Takaoka/Myst, Quennel Blackbird Stone/Stiller, Shannon De La Cruz/Queen Bee, and Devlin Fitz/Eight Man.

I extended my hand, feeling awkward as Donaghan shook

it.

"I'm Tabby. Tabitha. This is Dawn and Asher."

"Nice to meet you guys. So, do you want to play?"

Donaghan casually twirled a Frisbee on his index finger, one eyebrow arched expectantly.

Asher stepped forward. "Sure."

We followed Donaghan and his gang to a grassy area in the park and fanned out, standing in a circle as the game began. I jumped in the air, catching the Frisbee and throwing it back to Donaghan, who stood in front of me. He smiled at me for a second before throwing it to Asher, who tried a fancy move before tossing it to Dawn.

This is great. I thought. I couldn't keep the big smile off my face. I looked around; but for once, no one was staring at us. Here, we were safe, and I liked the feeling that it gave me. I met Donaghan's gaze again and felt a blush that had nothing to do with the heat creep up my neck. Devlin stretched and made a signal to Donaghan to end the game for lunch. Donaghan raised his eyebrows at the three of us again, and we eagerly followed them out of the park, none of us realizing that our cellphones were ringing frantically. I sat next to Asher at the restaurant, who had Dawn on his right as we gorged ourselves on hamburgers and Coke and playfully fought over what to order for dessert. Donaghan chuckled at a joke Devlin made, locking eyes with me. I shyly responded with a smile. Part of me thought it was crazy, flirting with a guy who was in high school, but somehow it felt good. Asher checked his watch and reluctantly he announced we had to go home, seeing that it was almost five o'clock. Donaghan and his friends looked disappointed but shook hands with us and offered to drive us back home. I climbed into the truck bed with my friends, scrunching next to Asher. Dawn laced her fingers with his as we pulled out of the restaurant's parking lot. I leaned back against the cab and wondered if we would see these guys again. The Children of Eris...what a weird name, I thought. Donaghan pulled off to the side of our street and let us out.

CHAPTER THREE

Donaghan flashed a parting smile. "You guys ought to come visit us sometime. We're over in Newport." he said.

Maiya scrawled a number on a slip of paper and handed it to Asher. "That's our number. Call us anytime, if you need anything." She put a slight emphasis on the last word and gave a friendly wink, causing Dawn to frown at her.

Asher grinned at her, oblivious to Dawn's look of jealousy. "Yeah, that sounds great. We will."

I nodded enthusiastically, feeling stupid as I did so.

"Yeah, that does sound good." I managed to say as I smiled thanks and headed down the street with Dawn and Asher flanking me. My senses suddenly went haywire, and I started running, smelling the smoke, and cursing myself for not seeing this before. I stopped short when I saw the police and neighbors milling around, including our next-door neighbors Davis and Annette Lockwood. Seeing the pair of stretchers holding two covered bodies, I started forward, stopping about a foot away. Unconsciously I reached out to touch one of the bodies, jerking back reflexively when Annette Lockwood told me not to touch anything.

"You can't touch anything." Annette said, though she looked more sad than angry.

"What happened?" I did not even recognize my own voice, part of me was half-convinced that I was not really here at all, it was a stranger having this conversation.

"There was a gas valve that exploded...caused the fire, and... they couldn't get out fast enough." Annette's voice broke and she turned away, her shoulders shaking.

Meanwhile, Asher was having words with Davis, who was apparently upset that we had not come home sooner.

"What happened?" Asher demanded.

Davis Lockwood shrugged his shoulders. "I don't know. Why didn't any of you answer your phones?"

"How were we supposed to know about this?" Asher's face twisted with anger.

Davis met Asher's furious gaze with his own. "You had a phone on you, why didn't you answer it? I called you about four times, nothing!"

"Well, we're not telepathic, sorry!" Asher finally lost his temper. I had never seen him quite this angry before, and for a minute I was afraid he would actually hit Davis. Dawn took his arm and gently pulled him away as Davis turned his back on us, going to where his wife stood and trying to comfort her. A police officer stepped away from his comrades and approached us. "Excuse me. Kids, I have to talk to you three." He gestured to me and my friends.

I mechanically nodded, answering his questions in a monotone voice.

"Where were you when this accident took place?"

"We were at the park. We...we met some other kids and we...lost track of time." I hated myself for how that sounded, so inadequate.

"Did the Wordens ever speak harshly of people, perhaps some neighbors that were particularly not fond of you three?"

"No. I mean, there were some people on this street who didn't like us very much. But...even they wouldn't take it this far." Even that failed to comfort me much, even though I knew it was true.

"The Wordens were your foster parents?"

"Yes." The past tense phrase made my heart ache.

"You three are wards of the state, is that correct?"

"Yes." I could barely talk for the lump in my throat, but I willed myself not to break down.

"What is going to happen now?" I tried to sound interested.

"Well, we'll have to call Social Services and see if we can find you guys new homes."

"Isn't there someone here who could take us in?" Dawn asked and frantically scanned the crowd. The officer looked around, asking aloud if anyone would be willing to shelter us for the night. After several agonizing minutes, Davis finally stepped forward. I forced myself to remain calm as we went inside to our temporary home; feeling everyone's eyes on us made me feel even worse. Davis was kind enough to show us where we could sleep before reminding us that Social Services would be coming to visit tomorrow.

"Are you guys hungry?" He asked.

Dawn tried hard to smile. "No, we already ate, thanks."

Asher made a noncommittal sound and headed upstairs. I found an empty bedroom upstairs and sat on the bed, finally allowing myself to cry. I straightened up when someone came to the door, but it was only Asher. He put an arm around my shoulders, asking if I would come down and eat.

"They said dinner will be ready at seven." Asher sighed. "How the hell can they expect us to think of food?"

I wiped my nose on a tissue. "I'll go if you guys will."

Asher patted me on the back and left for his room, while I went down to help Dawn set the table. The five of us ate dinner in silence; I tried to think of something to say and suddenly had an idea.

"Could you guys adopt us?" I asked, trying not to sound too eager.

Davis choked a bit on his drink and stared at me with a mixture of shock and pity. "No, Tabitha. We wouldn't be able to afford it."

"But, you guys –"

Davis shook his head. "Tabitha, please. Don't get your hopes up. Social Services will more than likely put you three in separate homes after this. I'm sorry...but you'll just have to take what you can get now."

I bit my tongue to keep from shouting at him and lowered my eyes back to my plate. I could hardly swallow anything more knowing we would only be here for a short while...and then what? What would happen to us? I tried to quiet my thoughts as I got ready for bed and let sleep overtake me. I was shaken awake barely two hours later by Dawn, who had a sack with food and extra clothes in it. Asher stood by the door, looking nervously at the foyer downstairs.

"Come on, we have to go." Dawn pulled urgently at my arm.

I blinked my eyes, not really registering what I was hearing. "What? What do you mean? Can't we just stay here for the night?"

"No, Social Services are coming tomorrow."

"Yeah, but —"

"We're not going to stay here forever."

"Dawn, could we please talk about this in the morning?"

"There is nothing to talk about. Tabby, come on —"

Dawn impatiently pulled me out of bed, throwing a spare outfit at me. I shook my head to clear it and hastily pulled on the jeans and shirt Dawn had given me. I slipped into my sneakers, quickly knotting the laces before putting on my jacket. I straightened up, fully dressed and demanded to know what the hell we were doing.

"They're going to split us up." Asher stepped into the room urgently. "You heard what Davis said down there, they said not to get our hopes up."

"But, Julianne and Carter –"

"That is over, Tabby." Asher had an almost hateful look on his face. "Damn it, we are wasting time."

"He's right, Tabby." Dawn was sadder than I had ever seen her. "We won't see each other again if we stay here."

I was shocked that it hadn't even occurred to me. But now, sitting alone with my friends in a strange bedroom, it suddenly became clear to me that our safe fairy tale lives had ended. If what Asher said was true, then we would have to take our chances and run while we could. I decided right then, anything was better than being sent to a different town or state without Dawn or Asher. I swallowed back the lump in my throat, following Asher as he led the way downstairs and quietly crept out the back door. We immediately turned north and headed up the street to the bus stop.

"So, any ideas where we're going?" I asked, not caring how idiotic that sounded.

"Newport." Asher set his jaw. "We can find these Eris guys and they'll help us."

"Did you bring –"

"Yes, I got it." Asher pulled out the slip of paper with Eris's number on it and showed it to me. My cellphone beeped suddenly, and I yanked it out of my pocket, blinking back tears as I saw the messages I had missed. A sudden rage came over me and I hurled my phone across the street, wiping my eyes as tears began running down my face. Dawn put a hand on my shoulder and reluctantly I forced myself to press on. I didn't want to dwell on what would happen when we found the Eris gang, I just hoped we could work something out.

Yeah, just for the next five years. The snide thought caused me to chuckle to myself, although there was really nothing funny about our situation. We walked quickly, huddling together to stay warm, since none of us were dressed for a cold night.

"S-stop." My lips were numb, and I was cold all over, but I hugged myself tighter and jerked my head backward. "W-we're being f-followed."

"By whom?" Dawn asked, shivering.

"I don't know." I could sense the person – people, I corrected myself, as I heard more footfalls. They definitely seemed human, I sensed, and yet, something in their presence didn't feel quite right.

"A-are they l-l-like us?" Asher stuttered hopefully.

I shook my head. "No, they're human, but…they don't feel right."

"Hey there." The lazy, drawing voice behind us made me jump in fright. A man, perhaps in his early thirties, leaned against the edge of the building, not twelve feet from where we were standing. I was amazed that the man (if he even was that) could sneak up on us like that without my hearing it. Two females flanked him, and two more males stood behind him. My insect sense told me there was definitely something weird about these people, something about their genetic makeup that didn't come off right. But no matter how hard I tried, I just couldn't figure out what it was. Later

I would assume it was the hungry gleam in their eyes, the way they seemed more relaxed than was humanly possible, on a subzero night like this. The fact that they didn't seem to feel the cold, even though Dawn, Asher and I were shivering so hard we could barely stand up. And I definitely didn't like the way these...people smiled even more widely at that fact. But right then all I could think was that I didn't want them near me or my friends. The three of us backed up, Dawn clenching one of our hands in hers. My eyes met hers briefly, the steady look in her gaze told me she would think of a plan. The quintet advanced, evil emanating from them in waves, their canines seeming to grow out over their lips. *Evil.* The word stabbed into my brain like a knife. That was it, that's why these five felt so wrong. The leader lunged at me. Without thinking I punched the man full in the face, lifting him off his feet and sending him flying back into the wall. He landed hard and didn't get up again. Dawn phased through one the females, rendering her shocked; Asher dived out of the second female's reach and rolled in a nearby puddle. The female snarled and swiped at him. Asher counter-attacked and his scales cut into her eyes. She screamed, clutching her bloody face in agony. I smashed her across the head and knocked her out, then did the same for Dawn's attacker. The other two males stood shell-shocked. One of them tried to speak. "What the fuck-"

"You guys aren't human." I cut him off, an insolent smile of my own spreading across my face. "And you know what? We aren't either."

"Amen." An unfamiliar male voice rang out. The two males seemed to recognize it, but before either of them could react, gunfire tore through both of them and, before my disbelieving eyes, turned them both into ash. Dawn had grabbed me, turning me intangible, though I vomited the second she let go of me, having never been used to solid objects passing through me. The newcomer, a handsome, stocky young man, leveled his weapons at us, demanding to know who we were. "More to the point, *what* the hell are you?"

Dawn's voice shook, but her eyes were strangely clear and steady. "We're mutants. I'm Dawn, and this is Tabby." She put a hand on my shoulder.

"That's Asher over there." Dawn pointed to Asher's dark fish-like form huddled in the corner behind the dumpster. "You can come out, Ace, he won't hurt us. Will you?" She asked, as an afterthought. The young man shook his head. Asher walked into the light, and the man nearly dropped his weapons, gawking at Asher's webbed hands and damp, scaly skin. Dawn explained what we could do the best she could, and Asher shyly requested to borrow the man's coat to dry himself off with. The young man peeled off his jacket and grudgingly handed it over.

"So, who are *you*?" I finally found my voice again.

He glared at me, but volunteered the basics: "My name's Darien, these freakbags-" he gestured to the unconscious people-

"...are vampires."

"That's why they turned to ash when you shot them?" Asher asked.

"Yeah." He turned and walked away, having decided we weren't a threat, but we followed him. Darien spun around, dark brown eyes flashing. "You got a death wish or what?"

I took a deep breath and coolly informed him that we no longer had a home and needed shelter. Darien scowled, clearly not happy about the situation, but grudgingly motioned for us to come with him. Darien climbed behind the wheel of a black '66 GTO,

Dawn and Asher took the back, I clambered into the shotgun seat. Darien started the engine, and I was amazed it didn't wake the dead with the roar it made. I was so engrossed in our unlikely and even more unwilling guardian that I didn't notice the other trio of people standing in an alley, watching us drive away. Had I turned around, I would have undoubtedly recognized them.

CHAPTER FOUR

Calvin, shorter and slightly thinner than the six foot-two blond Hector, lit up a cigarette, sharing his smoke with his rough-hewn, burly partner. Delia, five foot seven and slender, watched the powerful automobile pull away with the three freak youngsters inside. Hector spat, angry that they had let the children get away. "We should have mopped up those little mutants while they were fighting those other freaks."

Calvin shoved back his light brown hair and gave Hector a look of disgust for not being more controlled.

Delia, not disturbed in the least, gave her lover an eerily cold smile. "Be patient, Hector." She stroked his cheek with creepy intimacy. "Their time will come, just like their traitor guardians."

Hector gave an equally cruel smile and fiddled with a lock of her hair. Calvin turned away, a glint of jealousy in his eyes, already forming a sadistic plan.

****

Darien drove quickly and without apology or explanation as to where we were going. Despite my persistent questioning, he refused to speak to any of us. I only shut up when he threatened to stun me, brandishing a taser to prove it. Darien shoved the stun gun back in its holster and stepped even harder on the gas.

After several more screeching turns, he finally stopped at a rundown, clapboard dock house.

"There's a spare bedroom." He said curtly, and walked inside, leaving us alone. The three of us climbed out of the car, wearily locating the spare room and collapsing on the bed, too tired to worry about who slept where.

I woke up the next morning, somewhat unsettled to find Asher sprawled out next to me. I was doubly surprised to find that he and Dawn were holding hands, sound asleep. I sat up, stretching, thinking I would go and buy groceries today. Then, as I took in the unfamiliar surroundings I remembered where I was and what had happened, and that none of us had any money. I wandered through the house, glimpsing Darien's door and stopping at the kitchen when I smelled food. I peeked inside and caught sight of a man, grizzled and gray-haired, standing at the stove. Even from the doorway I could see the man's eyes were brilliant sky blue. My stomach rumbled and I gave a hearty sniff at the smell of bacon and eggs, never guessing that the man in the kitchen would pull a shotgun from out of nowhere and try to shoot me. But if I was unprepared for his reaction, the old man went ballistic, shooting like a maniac when he saw me start jumping around like an insect. Awakened by the shots, Dawn and Asher came running in. Dawn phased through my elderly attacker, and he collapsed on the floor, mouthing someone's name. Asher wrestled the gun away and took it back to the kitchen, setting it carefully on the table. Darien bolted from his bedroom, still in his nightclothes, his light brown hair tousled.

"What the hell did you *do* to my uncle?" He yelled, upon seeing the old man sprawled on the carpet.

"He tried to shoot me!" I shouted back. "Why didn't you tell him about us?"

Darien angrily picked his uncle up in a fireman's lift, carrying him to the couch and laying a pillow under his head with surprising tenderness. We waited until Darien's uncle woke up and then went to the kitchen. I threw myself into the chair on Asher's right, farthest from Darien and his uncle, whom Darien introduced as Aldrich St. Albans. Aldrich looked sorry he had shot at me, upon hearing Darien's hasty explanation that my friends and I were mutants. Asher, with Dawn on his left and holding her hand under the table, immediately started asking questions about the vampire quintet we had met last night.

"Vampires can climb walls like insects do. Like...you do." He said, with a meaningful, apologetic look in my direction.

"What else do vampires do?" Dawn asked coolly. She hadn't quite forgiven him for trying to kill me earlier, and she clearly didn't feel any remorse for literally almost giving him a heart attack.

Aldrich rubbed his head, fixing us with a hard stare. "They can see in the dark, heal themselves, and they have superhuman strength. Like your friend here." Aldrich pointed at me.

"Actually, I can't heal myself or see in the dark." I informed him, not liking being lumped in with evil beings.

"Well, you get the idea." Aldrich snapped.

"So do you use holy water, crosses, stuff like that?" Asher

asked.

Aldrich let loose a barking, derisive laugh. "Son, you need to get your old wives' tales straight. Hold up a cross or douse them with holy water, all vampires will do is laugh in your face."

Asher's face tightened slightly. "So how do you kill them?"

Aldrich suddenly became sober. "Silver, garlic, or sunlight. But black onyx will protect them from ultraviolet rays."

Aldrich's eyes looked strangely misty, as if he were remembering something painful. Dawn, Asher, and I each explained in turn what we could do, and Darien recounted the tale of how the four of us had met. Aldrich gave an impressed chuckle, Dawn finally smiled, and, truce declared, Darien went to fix breakfast. My stomach growled even louder: I looked at the clock and saw that it was almost nine o'clock. I eagerly wolfed down the plate of eggs and toast Darien set in front of me. Later that day, I located a battered pack of playing cards and the three of us engaged in several noisy games of Animal, Menagerie and Slap Face. We also learned how to use vampire weapons, despite our protests that we were perfectly capable. Aldrich treated us to a stern lecture that it didn't matter how gifted we were, he wouldn't

risk anything. Better to learn, he said, than to go out unprepared.

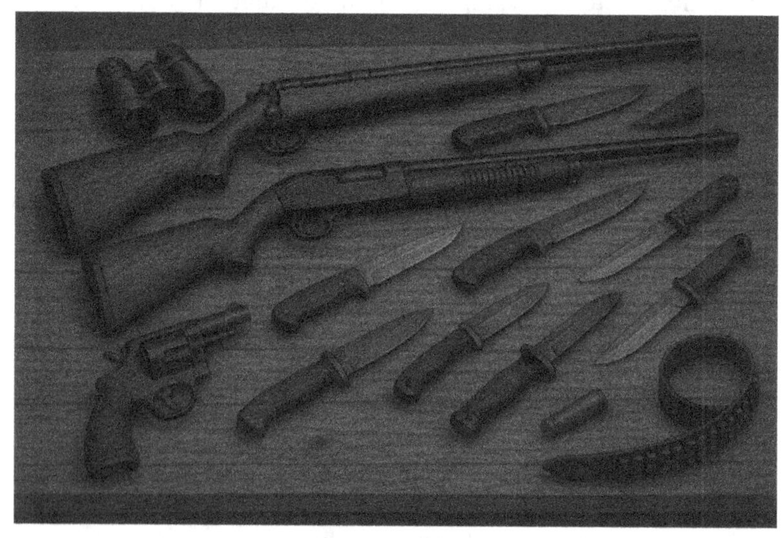

CHAPTER FIVE

AT THE EXTERMINATORS' LAIR, THE SAME MORNING

Reverend Angus Barstow, sixty, sat in his personal Garden of Eden, reading his newspaper, smirking at the sub-headline **COUPLE DISCOVERED DEAD IN WESTERLY, FOSTER CHILDREN ON THE RUN. NEIGHBORS REPORT THAT RUNAWAYS ARE MUTANTS.**

"We'll find them, Reverend." Delia's voice sounded reassuringly behind him, but she also sounded nervous. She knew, as one of the reverend's personal bodyguards, that he did not and would not tolerate failures. The stocky, silver-haired reverend merely grunted, taking a sip from his coffee cup. The Reverend fixed her with a steely stare. "Find those children, Delia. They know about that school that's being built for their kind."

Delia nodded, not letting her inner relief show. "Yes, sir." She gave a formal salute and turned to leave.

"Delia…"

"Yes, Reverend?"

A cruel smile had lit the old man's face. "Bring the redhead to me. Kill the other two."

Delia returned his cold grin. "Of course, sir." She walked out, flipping back her long ebony ponytail, a sinister plan forming in her head. She knew just how to flush the redhead out of hiding and make her want to find them.

****

THREE WEEKS LATER

Early afternoon, I sat munching mechanically on my BLT sandwich, a can of Root Beer by my plate, waiting impatiently for the others to return. Dawn and Asher, after sharing harsh words with Aldrich, had gone for a walk in the park to cool off. I noticed that they did spend a lot of time together, but I wasn't offended. I had long since started to notice their growing feelings for each other. Frustration gnawed at me as I gnawed at my sandwich; Darien and Aldrich had flatly refused our pleas to go after these

Exterminators, despite my warnings that more innocent mutants and their families would die if they didn't. Dawn had threatened that we would go after them ourselves, but we all knew otherwise because gifted or not, we wouldn't last long out there on our own.

I heard a scuffling by the front door and went to investigate. I saw a young blond man, late twenties, discreetly picking the lock and glancing nervously from side to side as though frightened of getting caught. Sensing that this man was not a threat, I went to greet him. He reacted with shock at seeing me here but accepted my invitation to come inside. He seemed paler than normal and a bit reluctant to smile, and I saw that he also had a black onyx ring on his middle finger.

"Are you a vampire?" I asked, just out curiosity.

The man lowered his eyes in unmistakable shame, fingering his ring. "Well...yes, but I'm also part human. My father had an affair with a vampire woman."

I examined him more closely, seeing that he had Aldrich's eyes. "Are you..."

He stiffened and seemed to sense my unasked question. "Aldrich St. Albans is my father. My name is Alain." To my surprise, his eyes filled with tears, which he quickly brushed away.

"My name's Tabby."

Alain smiled. "You're like me, aren't you?"

"What? No, I'm not-"

"No, I didn't mean you were a vampire. I meant you're just…not normal either."

I chuckled bitterly. "You're right, I'm not." To demonstrate that fact, I picked up a twelve-pack of soda, which was barely a feather in my hand, and hefted it on top of the fridge. I offered him a Root Beer, and soon we were trading stories. I found out that Alain and Darien, cousins by marriage, were the same age, twenty-eight, and that Alain was a human/vampire hybrid, the son of Aldrich and a female vampire. Alain had been forced out of his home after he'd turned thirteen, when his vampire side manifested itself. Darien's birth name was Andre Stratton, but he'd changed it when he was eighteen. Alain also had an older half-brother, Reece, who had formed his own monster-hunting organization called the Night Headers. I told Alain about my life: I was thirteen and a mutant, and how I'd lived in Westerly with my adoptive parents up until recently. I told him what little I could remember of my real parents, and my friends, what they could do, and how we'd lived in the same foster home for eight years. Suddenly the roar of a V-8 engine sounded in the distance, and I quickly swallowed the last sip of my soda.

"You'd better go." I said, pointing at the door

Alain got to his feet. "Don't tell them I was here."

"I won't."

I watched as Alain let himself out the back door and disappeared into the shipyards. Darien's car got closer and closer until I was covering my ears against the noise, wishing for once in my life that I didn't have such sensitive hearing.

CHAPTER SIX

I quickly picked up my sandwich as my friends, followed by Darien and Aldrich, walked in. Darien sat down, giving me a teasing look. "You'll choke one of these days if you keep eating like that."

Suddenly realizing how full my mouth was, I swallowed painfully and took a smaller bite. "You take big bites all the time." "Well, Darien's got a big mouth." Aldrich offered playfully, chuckling as Darien swatted at him. I smiled, thinking suddenly of Julianne and Carter. My smile faded and I forced those thoughts out of my head. I knew it would be a long time before I could think of them. Dawn's eyes looked a bit wet, and Asher looked like he had a stomachache, but I knew they were thinking of our foster parents too and hoping that they would get justice. Doubt crawled through my belly, cutting off my appetite and I left the kitchen. I fingered the garnet birthstone ring that Julianne had given me, the dark red color reflecting my runaway emotions. Tears ran down my cheeks and I tightened my lips, holding back a sob. Someone put a hand on my shoulder, and I was relieved to see it was Dawn. I didn't bother to wipe my eyes; somehow, I had never been ashamed of wearing my heart on my sleeve when around her. Asher came in holding two glasses of soda, one of which he handed to me. Seeing their rings made me feel better somehow, they were a reminder of the fact that we still had each other. I wiped my eyes and squeezed Dawn's hand, smiling at Asher. He smiled back, messing up my hair. I gave him a playful nudge and he tried to put me in a headlock. Dawn laughed and pretended to hold up a microphone, and soon I was wrestling with Asher like I used to eight years ago while Dawn acted as our commentator.

"And it's Insecta vs. Fisherman. It looks like Fisherman's got the upper hand this time, but oh there's Insecta making her move. Fisherman's getting his butt kicked, he's trying to get up but no, Insecta's got him! YYEEEAAAHHH!"

I heard the front door slam and knew Darien and Aldrich had just left.

Didn't even say good-bye. I thought bitterly as I listened to the car start up. Then I reminded myself that I couldn't expect these guys to get too close with us. But I couldn't deny that I had grown fond of them over the last three weeks and trusted them as I had Julianne and Carter. I got up and went outside, choosing a sunny spot to sit and look at the boats in the harbor. I watched as a couple went by on a white cigarette boat. They were smiling, holding hands, whooping with exhilaration. I watched enviously; those two people had no worries whatsoever. I wondered what that must be like, to live without fear. I closed my eyes; I would have traded a year of my life for a normal existence. I was so tired of hiding all the time…

I don't know how long I slept, but a couple hours later I woke up startled to find Dawn was standing over me.

"We're going shopping. Wanna come?" she asked Asher standing behind her.

I smiled and shook my head. Darien had, somewhat reluctantly, promised he would look after us until we found another place to stay. But still, I'd told myself before, a promise was a promise, reluctant or not. Besides that, Dawn and Asher had superpowers and could handle themselves. *They'd be all right.* I told myself.

Dawn grinned and said, "See you after," and left, Asher trailing behind waving back at me. I waved back at them exaggeratedly, grinning after him. I had no idea, though, that it would be the last time I would ever see the two of them alive.

CHAPTER SEVEN

I played card games, washed dishes, and did anything to keep myself occupied. Darien was out, Aldrich was God knew where, and I had no way to contact them. Around quarter of five, I decided to go look for my friends. I got a jacket and a flashlight and headed out after leaving a note for Darien and Aldrich. With each block, I grew more worried and angrier, by the time I reached the grocer's, I was raring to give Dawn and Asher a piece of my mind, not to mention Darien. But I never got the chance to talk to any of them; I smelled the smoke three blocks away and began to run. The scene was chaos: Fireman sprayed frantically, trying to stem the flames that greedily devoured the smallish corner store. Throngs lined the street, chattering amongst themselves, speculating on what had happened, whether it had been an accident or something deliberate. I saw no sign of my friends or the store's owner, though I looked until my eyes smarted and stung. I heard a snide remark from nearby and saw someone motioning towards me, but I was heedless. Somebody grabbed my arm from behind, jerking me around. Operating purely on instinct, I smashed the man in the face, sending him skidding backward into a parked car. A hush fell over the crowd. I realized, quivering with dread, that I had just exposed myself for a mutant. I was cold and sick and mad all at once and wished wildly for Darien. I knew that Dawn and Asher were dead, I knew it like I knew my own name. Another person threw a rock at me, and I ran, barreling into the nearest alley with a small mob on my heels. I leaped clear over the wall, running left and right until I finally lost them in an abandoned building. My eyes burned with unshed tears, which streamed silently down my face as I tried to hold my sobs back. *Where the hell was Darien?* I wondered furiously. I would have to wait here until morning and then sneak back to the dock house. I started to drift off when I heard voices outside. I jerked awake, trying to move quietly, and crept to the window to hear better. Carefully I looked over the windowsill, seeing three shadowy figures standing three feet away. Two men and a woman, by what I could hear.

"The other two are dead, and we killed those traitors who

raised the little freaks, why don't we just finish them all off?" One of the men spoke in a furious whisper. "I say mop up the trash while we got the chance."

The woman spoke. "Hector, we need Tabitha alive. Her friends were of no consequence. We only killed them to flush her out."

I felt as though I had been punched in the stomach. So, what happened to Julianne and Carter was no accident after all, and now Dawn and Asher were gone as well. The woman was speaking…about my mother and father! It took everything I did not have to run away at what I was hearing. Evidently my parents had been in an automobile accident after a very public renunciation of the Reverend Angus Barstow in Newport where he still lived…and who happened to be my grandfather! My dad's dad! *The reverend killed his own son…? How? Why?* Horrified at what I was hearing, I huddled on the floor, unseen by the trio who were talking about the deceased people I had known. *Mom. Dad. Julianne. Carter. Dawn. Asher.* The six names ran through my head like a chant, forcing me to sit still so I could hear everything they were saying. I learned that after Dad had fallen in love with a mutant, my mother, he had left home and was promptly disowned following a huge argument with the reverend. The trio left, their voices fading until I was alone with my thoughts. Sagging heavily against the wall, I finally fell asleep, my head full of monsters. Dreams of my friends, Julianne and Carter, haunted me hour after hour as I slept, the regrets in my heart like a knife. Darien could not take their place; he obviously didn't care enough to bother. Had I ever told any of them how much they had meant to me? I should have known, I should have told them.

CHAPTER EIGHT

I woke up with a start around dawn and got up. I searched the floor I was on and found some rope and a shovel, rusty as hell but still usable. Slowly I pushed the door open and crept cautiously back to the demolished store. I stepped gingerly through the rubble, my throat tightening when I saw a flash of bright gold to my left. I knew it was Dawn, as I drew closer, I saw the amethyst birthstone she had around her finger. That meant the one next to her was Asher, wearing his own topaz ring. I sat down hard, and before I could decide what to do my emotions boiled over and I started sobbing amongst the rubble, hugging myself against the chilly morning breeze. After a while, I got to my feet and seized Asher's corpse, dragging it more roughly than I intended. I pulled in a deep breath, struggling to be gentle despite the rage I felt as I tied the ropes around my friends' bodies, dragging them away from the ruined store. I walked for hours, in no particular hurry. Finally, I came to the outskirts of town and found a secluded, bushy area where I could bury them. I started digging the graves, my mind in turmoil, my heart wrenching with each clod of dirt I dug up. Saying a quick, silent apology, I pulled their rings off and put them on my own fingers. I wedged first Dawn, then Asher into the too short, semi-deep graves I had dug for them. With shaking hands, I carved the names DAWN CHANG and Asher ERMAN onto two rocks and laid them at the head of the graves. Unconsciously, I began mumbling, intending to say a eulogy, but what came out was a paraphrased verse from the Book of Zephaniah, 3:8: "'For my decision is to pour out upon them my indignation, all the heat of my anger, for in the fire of my jealous wrath all the earth will be consumed.'"

I knelt there in a hell all my own, twisting the three rings on my fingers. I finally collapsed, giving myself up to the pit inside me and eventually dozing off out of pure exhaustion. When I woke up next, it was mid-afternoon; and I was hungry, but not just for food: revenge. I rubbed my eyes, and after a final goodbye, started back for the dock house lair. I could only hope that God would be kind enough to look after my friends and not let anyone desecrate their graves.

Aldrich drove carefully through the streets, the sun threatening to make him fall asleep. Darien was fatigued but unable to rest; he leaned his head against the cool window, when something caught his eye.

"Aldrich, wait. Pull over."

"What is it?"

"I thought I saw a grave marker or something." Darien hopped out of the car and hurried to the spot. His legs buckled when he saw the name: Asher ERMAN. In shock, he looked at the other headstone: DAWN CHANG. Darien began to rock back and forth on his heels, his shoulders shaking. Aldrich put a hand on his nephew's shoulder, allowing both of them a moment. Silently, he helped Darien back to the car, not looking back at the graves as he started the engine and drove toward town.

****

The dock house was empty, for which I was thankful. I didn't want to face Darien or Aldrich yet; although I sincerely hoped Darien was holed up somewhere flogging himself, and Aldrich too, for that matter. I snacked on an apple and a slice of bread with cheese and then set about getting ready for my journey.

I put on the sturdiest boots I could find and located a battered

knapsack to hold all my things. Quickly I stuffed in food, a few

weapons, and money and grabbed a water bottle from the fridge.

I shouldered my pack and left, heading for the bus station…and to

my revenge. I sat down at the bus stop, drumming my feet absently

on the concrete. I checked my pocket, relieved to see I had the

right change for a bus fare. A metro bus pulled up and I glanced

at the sign to make sure that it was bound for Newport. I boarded

just as I heard a V-8 engine not too far away. I paid up front and

chose a seat near the back, far away from anyone else. I gripped

my bag tightly and stared fixedly out the window. My eyes were

hazel, green tinged with gold. I had never noticed that before,

funny. I saw the GTO pull up and caught a glimpse of Darien's

frantic face before I turned away. I tore the wrapping off a

sandwich, my growling stomach pulling me out of my thoughts.

Brushing the remaining crumbs off my lap, I slept fitfully until

one of the passengers reminded me that we had arrived in

Newport. I stepped off the bus, shrugging on my hooded jacket,

when suddenly someone jerked me into a secluded corner, ripping

my hood off. Darien stood there, looking terrified and sorry and angry all at once. I yanked my arm out of his grip and backed out of reach, bracing myself for a scuffle. Darien stared at my bag, at me armed to the teeth. "Where did you think you were going?"

CHAPTER NINE

"I don't think." I spat. "I *am* going. And where the hell were you last night?"

"Tabby, Jesus, I saw the graves. What happened?"

"Oh, so you *do* care?"

"YES, I CARE!"

"Don't bullshit me! You promised me, you looked me in the eye and said –"

"I KNOW WHAT I SAID!"

"You left me to face that mob alone!" I roared. "You didn't even bother to go look for Dawn or Asher! Did you even read my note?"

No, I realized, staring at the stricken look on Darien's face, he hadn't. He hadn't gone home at all that night. My anger began to cool, but I was far from forgiveness. "Well, well. 'He who upholds the good,' is having a moment. Is that what your name really means?"

Darien ignored my jibe, running his hands over his face. "What do you want me to say?"

"Try 'I'll help you take down these people, Tabby.' Say, 'I'll help you find your grandfather, Tabby."

Darien stared at me in total shock, tears staring to form in his eyes. "You mean humans? It was humans who…your grandfather…?"

"Yes, it was. Humans did it all." I sighed, for the first time pitying him. "Darien, I need your help. I'm going after these Exterminator guys."

"But they're humans. And your –"

"'They' killed my family and friends. And my grandfather told those people to do it." At the indecisive look on Darien's face, my temper started to boil, but seeing his tears, I couldn't bring myself to shout at him again.

"Look," I said more quietly, "You can stay if you want. But *I* am going." I walked off, leaving Darien to his thoughts. I trudged onward, thoughts of my friends bombarding me, like waves in the ocean: the three of us at five, in our new home, our first day kindergarten, grade school, when our powers manifested themselves at the ages of eight, all through middle school, the taunts, the threats, and still, we had stuck together after it all. But now no more; I was the only one left. I didn't even hear Alain come up until he tapped me on the shoulder. I spun around, stake in hand, then I saw it was just him. He looked sadder than I had seen him, and I knew he must have heard about Dawn and Asher.

"What will you do when you see these…people?" Alain asked, eyeing me worriedly.

I was surprised. "How do you know about that?"

He smiled crookedly, flashing his fangs. "I've been following you since our first meeting."

"You mean stalking me." I replied sarcastically.

He looked genuinely hurt. "No, I just mean…you're the first real friend I've had since…you know."

I softened considerably, realizing that Alain was a lot like me; he too had lost everything since becoming what he was now. I looked him straight in the eye. "Will you help me?"

He stared back, just as hard. "Yes."

I handed him a stake from my bag. "Do you have a weapon?"

He shook his head, pocketing the stake. "Don't you have a gun or something?"

"No. I don't like guns." I said. "Besides, I'm thirteen." He gave a sarcastic though understanding nod; we pressed on, not talking, though both of us had a million and one things on our minds. We reached the lair; my heart rate sped up; my fingers tightened on the stake in my pocket. A guard called Clifford was standing outside, a silver **E** badge on his chest that clearly marked him an Exterminator. Clifford saw us coming and raised his walkie-talkie. Alain moved forward, so fast even I couldn't believe it, and snapped the man's neck. He quickly seized the dead man's weapons, handing me the sword and pocketing the handgun. I couldn't help thinking as I hopped over Clifford's corpse, *one down.* I was one step closer to my revenge. Alarms blared, red lights flashed, and the Exterminators charged, with Hector, Delia, and Calvin in the lead. I was locked in a nightmare of guns, knives, and blood, fighting side by side with Alain. I waded in, gutting Calvin and tossing him across the room. He crashed through the window and fell three stories down, smashing his skull on the floor. Delia seized my wrist and tried to do the same to me, but I clung to the wall, flinging her twice as hard as out into space, where she met with a similar fate. She screamed all the way down, a scream that I savored. Hector roared and fired like a maniac, but I was too quick for him. I threw a knife that lodged in his throat and then struck him with a roundhouse punch that sent him skidding backward, where he struck the wall with such force that I could literally feel the floor shake. I braced myself again but then realized he couldn't get up; the impact had broken his spine.

I left him as was and threw myself at the next Exterminator, a woman named Elsa, who tried to stab me with a short sword. Obviously, she didn't like guns either. Too bad, because she wouldn't survive this night…none of them would, I silently promised myself that.

CHAPTER TEN

Our swords drew sparks; I was amazed at the strength in her body. Spinning and slashing, I managed to get the upper hand; and she became desperate, her blade cutting my arm. I countered and shoved my sword into her stomach, impaling her. Alain was locked in combat with a male Exterminator named Bartholomew, fighting fiercely but losing; I saw a female called Charlene about to shoot him with a silver bullet. I sprinted forward, screaming a warning, but before I could do anything, gunfire sounded, both Exterminators dropped to the floor, shot through the chest. Aldrich St. Albans stood clutching a gun, with Darien at his side.

"That's my son, bitch." Aldrich snarled, kicking the dying Charlene in the head to finish her. He and Alain shared a brief affectionate look before tangling with the remaining Exterminators Juana, Enrico, and Giles. I saw my chance and ran to find the reverend. Room after room I passed by; suddenly an arm shot out, dropping me like a sack of potatoes. I glimpsed gray hair and piercing hazel eyes before crumpling in a dazed heap. Angus Barstow, my grandfather, my betrayer, stood above me. His eyes, so much like mine, were shining with malice.

"Well done, Tabby."

Rage soared in me; I lunged, stake at the ready, but he countered with such quickness that I faltered. Amazingly, while he beat and kicked me, he began to recite a quote from the Bible: "'I have laid waste their streets, so that none walks in them, their cities have been made desolate, without an inhabitant. And I will cast you on the ground.'" He gave me a final kick at the last sentence; my ribs, back, and stomach aching with bruises. The reverend smirked, cocking his gun, never knowing that I was playing possum the entire time. I lashed out, kicking away the arm that held the gun. Then, to my shock, Darien, with Giles on his heels, came charging in. Darien jumped on the reverend, knocking him down before being pulled away by Giles. I seized the gun and began kicking the reverend, reciting my own Bible verses: "'You are cursed with a curse, for you have robbed me. Because you have raged against me and your arrogance has come to me, I will turn you back on the way by which you came."

I raised the gun, soaked in blood and sweat, intending to finish him off, but something held me back from doing so. I thought of everything he had done: Dawn and Asher, Julianne and Carter, Mom and Dad. The parents I never knew, the friends I always thought I would have, the guardians who had loved me like a daughter.

He stared at me, the mad reverend, the ardent hater, my grandfather…*my grandfather. My flesh and blood.* That was it, that's all that kept me from pulling that trigger and sending him to the hell that he had envisioned for me and my kind. I grabbed my grandfather's collar and jerked him on his knees, forcing him to crawl out. A few feet behind, Darien followed, his clothes heavily smeared with Giles's blood.

"Are you alright?" Darien asked suddenly. I jumped a bit, not expecting his concern.

"Yeah, I'm –" Two tears rolled down my face and I sniffed before I could stop myself. Darien put a hand on my shoulder, but I couldn't bring myself to look at him. He pulled a tape recorder from his pocket, saying he'd gotten Reverend Barstow's confession on it. Aldrich had also found files he'd kept on everyone who was thought or known to be a mutant. They had found enough evidence to put him in jail, perhaps for the rest of his life. Darien and Aldrich tied the reverend up outside and put him in their car. I stood and watched a few feet away, never taking my eyes from my grandfather's hateful stare. Alain helped me toss gasoline around the building and set it on fire. He gave me a brief hug before climbing into the backseat. Darien looked at me expectantly, with a hint of a plea in his gaze, but I only stared at him. Darien's face twitched; I saw the sorrow in his eyes and felt a stab of remorse, but the best I could give him was a fleeting, grateful smile. Darien nodded quietly and drove off with Aldrich and Alain, who waved at me before they disappeared around the corner, leaving me alone. Hours later, as the fires roared distantly, I trudged down the very same street I had been terrorized on by Hector, Delia, and Calvin, the three who had been surveying my house. After killing off every member of Reverend Barstow's contingent, I knew I should have felt something: sadness, remorse, guilt, even. But all that I felt was a deep and profound peace. I walked slowly down the dark streets, huddling against the chill

Rhode Island wind. The night was quiet, but for the first time in

my life, I wasn't afraid.

ABOUT THE AUTHOR

Tessa Rice is a science fiction author based in Kailua-Kona, Hawaiʻi, whose work blends dystopian futures, supernatural suspense, and deeply human themes. Diagnosed with Asperger's Syndrome, Rice channels her unique perspective into stories that explore resilience, identity, and transformation.

A graduate of West Hawaiʻi Community College, Rice has participated in numerous writing groups and workshops to hone her craft. Her debut series, the *Eternus Trilogy*, introduces readers to a world where a teenage girl with elemental powers confronts authoritarian control in a society known as Celebrus Natio. The trilogy is noted for its vivid world-building and complex characters.

In 2024, Rice released *The Sydney Wilkins Trilogy*, a dark fantasy series that follows an eleven-year-old girl navigating family turmoil and supernatural threats. This work delves into themes of love, loss, and resilience, showcasing Rice's ability to intertwine emotional depth with thrilling narratives.

Beyond her novels, Rice is an advocate for aspiring writers, offering advice on balancing creative pursuits with daily life. She emphasizes the importance of perseverance and authenticity in storytelling.

Also from Stone Compass Press

Maui Vortex Field Guide
(Zach Royer, 2019. Also available as a Kindle eBook.)

Apocalyptic Revelations: The Emergence of Earth's Spiritual Awakening
(Sean McCleary, 2019)

Metaphysical Revelations: Information on the Dawning of a New Age
(Sean McCleary, 2018)

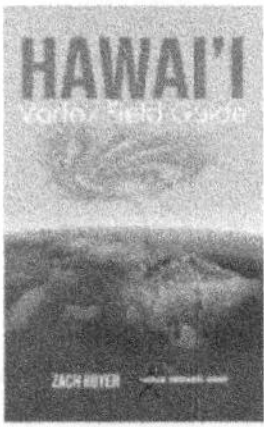

Hawai'i Vortex Field Guide
(Zach Royer, 2014. Also available as a Kindle eBook.)

Pyramid Rising: Planetary Acupuncture to Combat Climate Change
(Zach Royer, 2012)